This
book is
dedicated to

SPIKE Honey Louis

and their **shoes.**

Text copyright © 2000 by Bernard Lodge
Illustrations copyright © 2000 by Katherine Lodge
All rights reserved under International and
Pan-American Copyright Conventions.
Published in the United States by
Random House, Inc., New York
First published in Great Britain in 2000
by David & Charles Children's Books.

www.randomhouse.com/kids

Library of Congress Catalog Card Number: 00025914

In loving memory of Dracula

Thank you to

everyone at
David & Charles

Printed in Belgium
September 2000   10 9 8 7 6 5 4 3 2 1

RANDOM HOUSE and colophon are registered trademarks of Random House, Inc.

Shoe Shoe Baby

by **Bernard Lodge**

illustrated by
Katherine Lodge

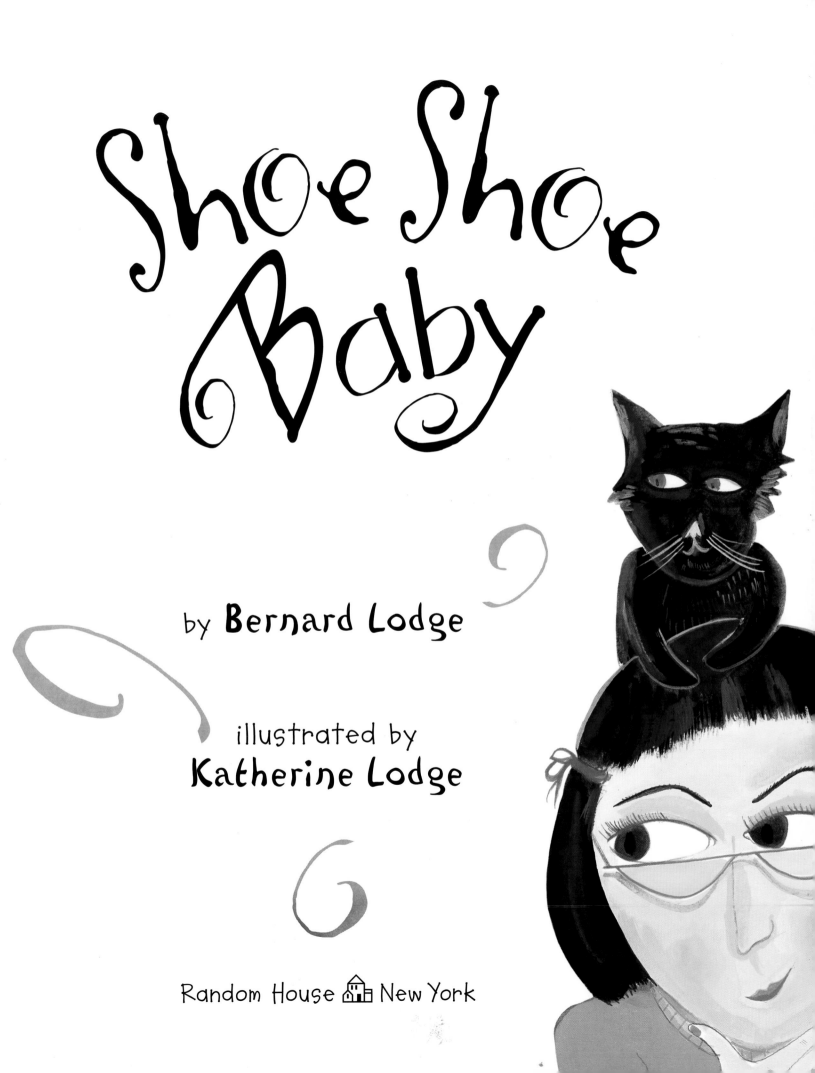

Random House 🏠 New York

Hello!

My name is **Shoe Shoe Baby.**

I come from a great family

of shoe-mad shoe people.

Grandma Cloggy made clogs from logs.

Cousin Horseshoe Hogan made shoes for haughty horses.

Uncle Toecap invented shoes that floated
. . . until they sank!

And here's my shop.
Like me, it's called
Shoe Shoe Baby.

SHOE SHOE BABY

It's the best shoe shop in town,
so you can't miss it. I sell every
kind of shoe you can think of,
and some you wouldn't even dream of.
It's open **seven** days a week, and last
week I had **seven** very weird customers.

On Monday morning, it was **Conchita** from Costa Rica.

"I'm homesick," said Conchita. "I miss the sun and the sea and the waving palms."

"Then **these** are for you," I said. I opened a shoebox, and Conchita's eyes lit up.

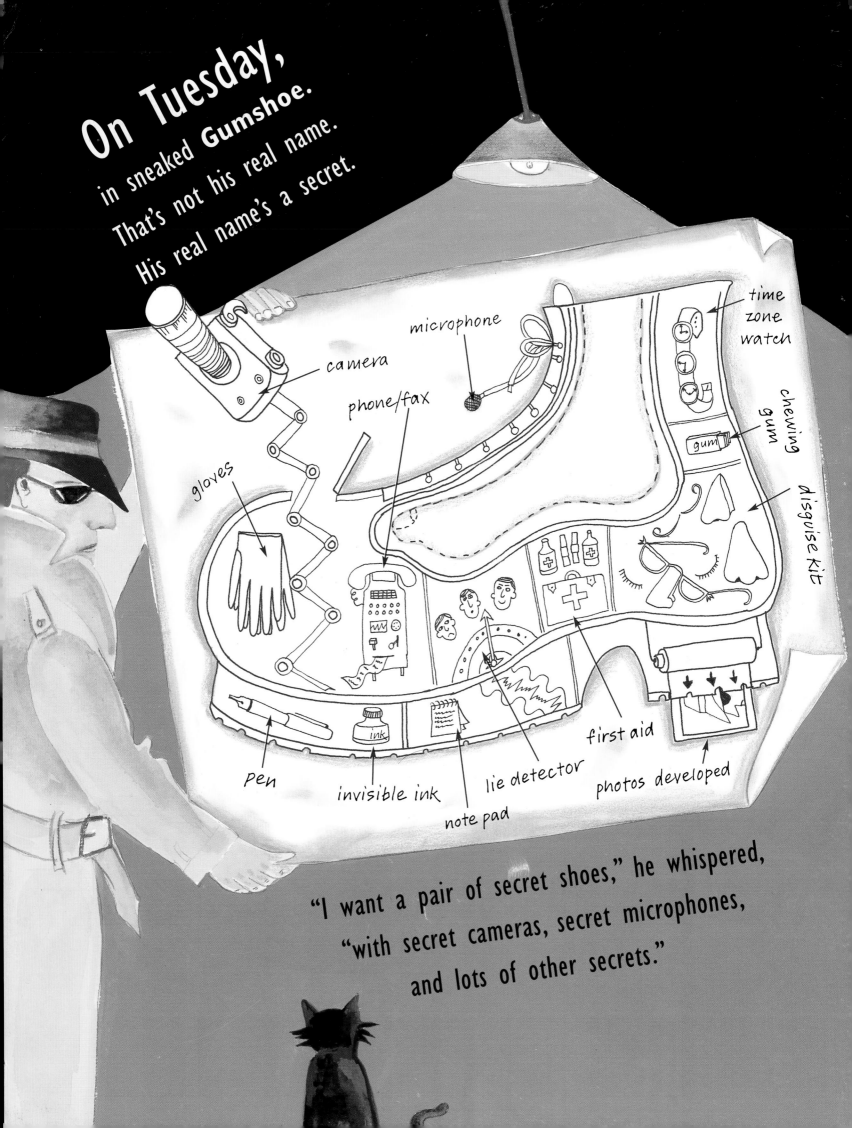

On Tuesday,
in sneaked **Gumshoe**.
That's not his real name.
His real name's a secret.

camera

microphone

phone/fax

gloves

time zone watch

chewing gum

gum

disguise kit

pen

invisible ink

ink

note pad

lie detector

first aid

photos developed

"I want a pair of secret shoes," he whispered,
"with secret cameras, secret microphones,
and lots of other secrets."

On Wednesday, I got a call

from the famous ballerina **Popova.**
"Can you pop over?" she pleaded.
"I've danced all week, so my toes
are tired and my heels are heavy.
Have you got anything to put
a spring in my step?"

"How about springs?" I suggested.

That night, her leap was so high they had to raise the chandelier!

On Thursday, little Bill Flinn

came in. He was **cranky.**

"My brother Tim is taller than me," he sulked.

"Of course he is," I said. "You're only
five years old and Tim is nearly ten."

"But I want to be **big**
like Tim **now!**" said Bill.

So I sold him a pair of stilt-built shoes.
Now Bill is bigger than Tim.
But what happens if Tim buys
some stilt-built shoes too?

Friday was funny.

In came **Cocomo,** the saddest clown in town.

"Kids don't laugh at me anymore," he sighed.

"Cheer up, Cocomo," I said. "Try on these wacky shoes. They **quack** as you walk."

"Hey—they're great!" grinned Cocomo.

quack!

quack!

He walked,
quacking happily,
around the shop . . . till he fell over.
"Oh no!" cried Cocomo. "Your wacky
quacky shoes trip me up!"
But then he heard the children laugh.
And Cocomo laughed. And I laughed too.

Saturday was

rodeo day, so in came
Tex from New Mex.

"I need some speedy boots,"
said Tex.

"For horse riding?" I asked.

"Nope," said Tex.
"I'm scared of horses."

"For your motorcycle?"
I suggested.

"Nope," said Tex.
"Ain't got one. Can't
stand the smell."

But on **Sunday** night I closed the shop and climbed into my queen-size shoe bed, and I slept like a clog, and I dreamt of an island . . .

. . . it was lovely **Barefoot Island,**
where no one could wear shoes,
or buy shoes, or ever, ever sell shoes . . .

Time to open shop!